RIVER
of
BLOOD

Felix Bogarte

Spooky Moon

First published 2003 by Spooky Moon Publishing,
an imprint of Books Noir Ltd

© 2003 Books Noir Ltd

www.booksnoir.com

Text written by Jimmy Docherty, based on a story
by Mhairi McDermaid

ISBN 1-904684-06-8

Printed and bound in the UK

Contents

Chapter 1

An Awful Discovery

On each side of the River Linn in Linchester lie a history and a derelict reputation that once placed the city proudly on the world-wide map. The reputation was for building the finest ships in the world, a reputation struggling to keep its head above water now.

Most of the shipyards have closed, the sound of hammering and heavy industry long fallen silent, and the warehouses built to accommodate the burgeoning shipping trade have been left to rot.

At night the rats head out into the moonlight to feast on the remains of whatever they can find, running and scurrying, nibbling and gnawing, under the cover of darkness . . .

*

The early morning mist rolled long and straight down the centre of the river, spreading out towards the dry land on each side, wisping and twirling, creeping and dancing.

The moon fought hard to light the black charred remains of derelict warehouses and factories that stood alone in the darkness, yet close enough together to hide in each other's shadows.

In the distance stood Lovell's Shipyard, a small shipyard whose task it was to service and refit old ships in dire need of a new face, one of the few shipyards that remain.

High up, on giant holding stands out of the water, sat the ship the *Kurdler*, with its grey flaking paintwork and portholes surrounded by rust.

The mist slowed. It stopped spreading out. Instead it just slowly rolled towards the ship like a vulture creeping up on a seemingly dead animal, not sure if it might turn and attack.

Then it stopped. Dead.

On some scaffolding at the foot of the *Kurdler* a small group of workers were already at work. A large hole had been made in the hull of the ship near the bottom for the workers to climb inside and replace any sheet metal that had come loose. Inside, two welders were already at work ripping off some metal cladding and prising off eighty-year-old rusted rivets that held the hull together.

One of the workers managed to force open the sheet of metal far enough to squeeze his body through behind it.

"Can you see anything in there, Charlie?" asked his workmate, still pulling at the metal on the other side.

"No, it's too dark," replied Charlie. "Pass me through a torch."

Charlie's workmate reached into his tool bag and pulled out a torch. Stepping over the puddles of water and dodging the never-ending trickle of water from the roof, he passed the torch through to Charlie.

"I'll tell you something, it doesn't half stink in there, mate," he said as Charlie took the torch from him. "It smells as if something's died, a long time ago."

Charlie pressed the "on" button on the top of the torch. For a short second the light flamed but then flickered briefly before fading back fast to darkness.

"The batteries are dead," said Charlie. "We need new batteries."

"Sometimes it does that. Just give a it a little bash and it should come on," replied his work-mate.

Charlie tapped the torch lightly on the side of the hull, then pressed the button. The torch flickered momentarily, then the light came on.

"That's it now," shouted Charlie, as he quickly shone the torch around.

It didn't take long for him to realise that the walls were very close together.

"This is weird," he said to his workmate, who had by now returned to his own task of stripping the metal at the other side of the hull. "It's as though this part of the hull was closed in for a reason, as though they wanted something blocked here."

"Can you see anything else?" asked his workmate.

"Hold on," Charlie replied, "there's a corner here that I haven't checked."

Slowly Charlie moved towards the dark recess of the corner, the light from his torch gradually brightening the walls as he drew closer. Faint scratch marks appeared down each side of the walls at the rivets, as though something had been scratching to get out.

Charlie paused for a second to look at the scratch marks. He held up his hand and noticed that the sizes of the marks fitted perfectly the size of his fingernails.

A cold sweat started to form on his forehead. Breathing heavily and scared at what he might find, he shone the torch around the wall, past the scratch marks into the corner. The light came to rest on a human skull. Its eye sockets were deep and black, and its jaw was stuck open. The body of the skeleton wore an old dirty worn suit from the 1920s.

As Charlie turned to run, his terrified screams bounced off every wall in the ship and echoed around the darkness of the shipyard outside. He dropped the torch, sending it spinning to the wet ground.

Ripping back the metal opening with his bare hands, Charlie squeezed his body back through to his workmate on the other side. His screams continued as he ran petrified through the hull and out into the yard.

Outside, the mist started to move backwards, creeping eerily away from the ship, like a frightened animal in retreat, too scared to turn and run, too afraid to take its eyes off its enemy. Like a vacuum it moved, pulling back from inside the vast black warehouses and buildings. The rats inside ran screaming, clambering over each other in desperate attempts to get away from the ship. Even the rats knew something deadly was in the air.

As the mist retreated back up the river, black clouds appeared, low and loud, rumbling across the sky towards the *Kurdler*.

Like black plumes of smoke, they advanced from out of nowhere, low over the Linn, to embrace the evil that had just been uncovered.

The torchlight continued to twirl and spin inside the hull, dancing around the walls and illuminating the skeleton as it passed. As it slowed, it lit the scratch marks on the walls, the old brown suit, and a small black briefcase beside the remains of the skeleton. Then it stopped, on the skull, and a small simple message scratched into the wall behind by human fingers.

It read, "Kilroy was here".

Chapter 2

Kilroy Strikes Again

It didn't take long for the heavens to fall. Only hours.

It was difficult to tell where night-time ended and morning began. The skies were still filled with black clouds. Blocking out all but small traces of daylight, they just hung in the air, as though there had been a large explosion and the smoke clouds had refused to disappear.

It had been only a matter of hours since the skeleton remains were found in the hull of the ship *Kurdler*. In fact, most of Linchester was still waking by the time Henry Hardy climbed the long sandstone stairs to the Art Gallery to start work early.

Henry was the first person to arrive in the building, and as he walked through the large main entrance into the vast foyer of the gallery, he was immediately aware that something didn't feel quite right. He stopped and had a look around. His eyes shifted nervously between the ancient Roman sculptures that separated the exhibition halls and the large canvas paintings that hung proudly on the walls, but he could see nothing. It was a cold morning, but for some reason the interior of the art gallery seemed a lot colder than normal.

Henry turned and walked to the end of the foyer to the large marble stairs that led up to his office. As he got closer to the stairs he heard a faint whisper echo through the large halls of the museum.

"Henry," the whisper said, soft and sinister.

Henry spun around, but the museum was eerily silent. There was no noise, and nobody there.

"Who's there," Henry shouted back down the foyer from where he had just come. His own words bounced off the walls and came straight back to him.

Still there was silence.

"I know there's somebody in here," he yelled. "This isn't funny."

He waited a couple of seconds for a reply, half expecting one of the night security staff to emerge from behind a statue somewhere, laughing, but no one answered.

Suddenly, a loud thumping noise could be heard from the top of the stairs. It became louder and louder, until Henry realised that whatever was making the noise was coming down the stairs straight for him. The noise kept getting louder and louder, and nearer and nearer, until a small rubber ball appeared from around the curved stairs and bounced down the stairs directly in front of Henry, one at a time, slow and loud, the noise of each bounce ricocheting off the walls around him. The ball reached the bottom stair and stopped directly between Henry's feet.

"I've had enough of this," yelled Henry angrily. "Show yourself!"

"You don't know me, do you?" came the whispered reply.

The sound of the whisper made Henry's blood run cold. "No, I don't," he replied, spinning around desperately looking for a face. "Who are you?"

"I knew your father," the whisper said. "He might have mentioned me. My name is Kilroy."

The name was vaguely familiar to Henry, although he couldn't quite remember from where.

"I worked in the shipyards many years ago," the whisper continued, "at the same time as your father."

A sudden terror filled Henry as he remembered the story his father used to tell him about the legend of Kilroy.

"What do you want from me?" Henry asked, trying hard to hide the fear in his voice, but the gallery was once again silent.

Henry looked around, unsure if whatever it was, was still there.

The silence was suddenly shattered with the spine-chilling, sinister soft tones of the whisper. "Revenge," it said.

The clatter of Henry's briefcase dropping to the floor echoed all around him as he ran as quickly as he could to the door, as fast as his legs could carry him towards the large double doors that led outside. Before he reached them the doors swung shut with an almighty clatter, locking Henry inside. Once again the gallery was totally silent. A cold wind swept through the large halls, down the stairs and along the foyer to where Henry was standing with his back to it, and stopped directly behind him.

"Why me?" Henry asked, too afraid to turn around.

"Why you?" came the whispered reply. "Because of what your father did."

Henry took a deep breath and wiped the sweat from his forehead. He slowly turned around to face what was behind him. As he turned he saw what it was that had been whispering to him. It was a large, almost transparent, demonic looking spirit, with a huge bony head that was too big for its small willowy body. Its shoulder bones were pointed and thin and its arms long and slender, with long crooked fingers on each hand.

"You're Kilroy?" asked Henry quietly, not needing an answer.

"Yes," replied the spirit, "and your time is up." With that he lifted his long thin arms up to the sky. The walls started to shake, paintings fell from the wall, sculptures fell from pedestals and smashed on the cold stone floor. He opened his mouth wide and an earth-shattering shriek filled the air. Then slowly he turned to Henry.

Henry closed his eyes.

*

Across the city Paul Alexander was just waking. And snoozing. And waking again. Paul had trouble getting up in time for school, so every morning he would set the alarm on his mobile phone, then hit the snooze button every time it beeped until eventually his mother would have to come in and wake him.

Except this wasn't an ordinary morning; this wasn't a school day; this was the first day of Paul's summer holidays.

Paul threw back his duvet and sleepily pulled himself to the side of his bed. His legs dangled over the side but not right to the bottom in case something grabbed his ankles from under the bed. Paul was the kind of ten-year-old who believed every ghost story he'd ever heard. No matter how ridiculous it sounded, he always found a way of convincing himself that it was the truth.

He rubbed the sleep from his eyes, yawned

loudly and jumped from his bed into the middle of the floor, careful so that his feet wouldn't touch the floor around his bed.

"Didn't get me this morning," he said defiantly to the imaginary monster under his bed, feeling proud of himself for evading its imaginary clutches for another morning. Suddenly his mobile started to beep, startling him slightly and making him jump.

Paul picked up his phone and noticed a text message from his best friend, Tommy Johnstone. "Good timing as ever," he muttered sarcastically to himself as he opened the message. It read, "GET UP WE R GOING 2 THE RIVER. A BODY WAS FOUND. DON'T B L8."

"I'm not going anywhere near that river," Paul thought to himself. Then another message arrived on his phone from Tommy: "YES U R, GET U'R GEAR ON." Tommy always had a way of knowing exactly how Paul would be thinking.

Paul threw his phone on to the bed. "You go if you want, Tommy Johnstone," he said, "but personally I think you're off your head, so I'm staying put."

"Go where?" a voice asked.

Paul turned around to see his mother, Helen, standing in the doorway holding a pile of clean laundry.

"Nowhere," Paul replied, not wanting to tell his mother that sometimes he played down at the river.

"And are you going nowhere?" his mother asked, quizzing him like mothers do.

"Yes, I'm going nowhere," Paul replied.

"Good, you can cut the grass then."

"I—I can't, Mum," said Paul, the look of dread at having to cut the grass etched all over his face. "I'm going somewhere."

His mother looked at him a little confused: "You just said you were going nowhere."

"Yes, I know," retorted Paul, "but nowhere is in fact somewhere."

"Well, where is it?" asked his mother with a very puzzled expression on her face.

"It's anywhere," Paul replied, marching past her into the hallway and towards the stairs. "I can't talk now, Mum. I've got places to go and people to see. I'll be back later. We can talk some more then."

"Paul, wait," shouted his mother, but by the

time she reached the stairs Paul had already disappeared out of sight.

His mother turned and walked back into Paul's room, dumping the pile of clean clothes on to his bed. Carefully she folded each item and placed it into his drawers. She was almost finished by the time she heard Paul come back into the room and stop in the middle of the floor.

"Where did you get to before you realised you still had your pyjamas on?" she asked without turning around.

"The end of the street," Paul replied.

Chapter 3

Enter Jack Angel

"What are you, a man or a mouse?" said Tommy Johnstone cheekily to Paul.

As Tommy stood at the side of the Linn River, the water behind him seemed to be flowing in a different direction from normal, as though it was moving away from the *Kurdler*, which could be seen farther down the river, hoisted high out of the water in its dry dock. It had been only two days since the skeleton had been found, and the weather hadn't changed one bit. The normally bright daylight was absent. Instead, dullness was present throughout the whole of the city. It was as though the weather was somehow frozen at 5am, just at the point where it starts to get brighter but still not bright enough for the streetlights to go off.

This did not go unnoticed to either Paul or Tommy, but where Paul was timid and more easily frightened, Tommy was forceful and brave. Sometimes too brave, and most times too forceful.

"You can say what you like, Tommy," replied Paul to his best friend's cheeky remark, "but something's very weird here. There's definitely something in the air. I can sense it, so I ain't going near that ship."

Tommy's look at Paul was slightly bewildered. "What's wrong with you," he asked. "This is the most exciting thing that's happened around here in years."

"Exciting?" Paul replied, as though he couldn't quite believe the stupidity of Tommy's last statement. "There's nothing exciting about a skeleton."

Tommy just shook his head. Although they were both best friends they were exact opposites of each other in almost every way.

Paul walked to the side of the water. As he peered over the edge into the murky depths he noticed that he did not have a reflection. The light was too dull and the water was too dense to reflect anything. It didn't look like water, more like sludge.

23

"I heard, when they found the skeleton it was covered in rats that had eaten away all the flesh on the man, right down to his bones," said Tommy, trying his hardest to spook Paul, "and the walls were covered in scratch marks where he'd been trying to get out."

"You're right. That is very exciting," said Paul brightly, "if you're a total weirdo."

Tommy laughed and turned to face the *Kurdler*. He could see crows circling over the top of it. He was so fascinated by the sight of the spooky old ship that he didn't even hear the car that drove up behind them. It was a long black car, with blacked-out windows and a bonnet that seemed to go on forever. It pulled up at the side of the water, just behind Paul and Tommy. As Tommy eventually turned to look, the door of the car was thrown open and a tall, elderly, thin man stepped out. He was wearing a blue pin-striped suit and a long blue overcoat with a hat, like a detective from an old black and white movie.

"Hi there," said the man in an American accent. "My name is Jack Angel."

Paul and Tommy both looked at each other.

They had heard an American accent before, but this was the first time it was talking directly to them. Not only did the man look like an old detective but he talked like one too.

"I wonder if you boys could help me," Jack continued. "I'm a private investigator from New York, and I'm over here working on a case."

"Does this have anything to do with the skeleton in the ship?" Tommy asked eagerly.

Jack gave a little smile. "Yes it does," he replied, "and the body that was found in the Art Gallery as well."

Paul started to feel uncomfortable. He knew not to talk to strangers, and he didn't like talking about skeletons and dead bodies.

"What body?" asked Tommy, who by now was starting to ask questions like a little detective himself.

"A man was found crushed under a large sculpture," replied Jack.

"How do we know you're a private detective," asked Paul, quizzing the American.

"I'll show you," said Jack, as he took out his wallet from inside his coat.

The wallet was old and worn. He flipped it open so that Paul and Tommy could see what was inside. There were some American dollars and a small card with a picture of Jack and the words "City of New York Registered Private Detective".

Paul felt a little more at ease after seeing the man's identification but was still a bit unsure as to how they could help him. "How exactly can we help you?" he asked, looking more than a little confused.

"It's quite simple really," answered Jack. "I need a couple of streetwise kids who know this city and can show me how to get to where the next bodies are going to show up."

Tommy's eyes opened wide. He was both startled and excited at the same time. The chance to help a real detective solve a case was too good for him to pass up. "Other bodies?" he asked, not quite sure if he wanted to know the answer.

"Yes," said Jack. "I believe the skeleton in the ship and the body at the art gallery were linked, and I believe there will be more deaths before too long."

Paul took a step back. Unlike Tommy, helping to solve grizzly crimes was not his idea of fun.

"How are they linked?" Tommy asked.

"Well, beside both bodies they found something written on the wall. It said 'Kilroy was here'," replied Jack.

"You see that written on walls all over the place," said Paul knowingly, believing he had just uncovered a hole in Jack's evidence.

"Yeah," Tommy continued. "I bet they even write it on walls in America!"

The sight of Paul and Tommy so adamant that they were right made Jack laugh out loud a little, something that did not go down well with either of the boys.

"You are both absolutely right," said Jack.

This shock confession wasn't what Paul and Tommy were expecting. Both seemed even more confused now than ever.

"But do you know the story of this Kilroy?" Jack asked them both.

Paul and Tommy looked at each other with blank expressions on their faces, then turned back to Jack and shrugged.

"I think we should have a little sit-down,"

said Jack, taking off his overcoat and laying it on the bonnet of the car.

Paul and Tommy walked to the side of the river and sat down, dangling their legs over the side above the murky waters below. Jack sat down beside them.

"The legend of Kilroy goes a long way back," Jack said to them. "Kilroy was a man who was a horrible ship inspector. Not many guys liked him. In fact, nobody liked him at all. He was the type of guy who used to find faults with a ship when there weren't any."

Paul and Tommy sat quietly listening to every word that Jack said.

"'Way back years ago there used to be a lot more ships being built on this river, so it was difficult for Kilroy to remember which parts of ships he had inspected and which parts he hadn't. So to remind himself he would write the words 'Kilroy was here' on the wall whenever he inspected an area of a ship."

"Ah," said Tommy, suddenly realising, "so that's where it comes from."

"Yeah," replied Jack. "The story goes that one day he really upset a group of men who were working on a ship, and those men chased him around the ship until they finally cornered him right down in the hull."

"So what happened next?" Paul asked anxiously.

"I don't know for sure," replied Jack. "What I do know for definite is that Kilroy was somehow trapped in an air pocket that was welded shut, but I don't know if it was an accident or whether it was done on purpose."

The thought of Kilroy being trapped in the hull and scratching desperately to get out made Paul's blood run cold. He looked at the *Kurdler*, which was farther upriver, sitting menacingly high out of the water.

"The name of the ship was the *Kurdler*," said Jack, although neither of the boys needed to be told the name of the ship.

Jack continued: "During World War Two that ship was used to carry American soldiers to different battles all over Europe, and very often they would complain that at night they could hear the sound of a man screaming and wailing and scratching and banging, the sound of the trapped Kilroy."

"So how come you know so much about all of this?" Tommy asked suspiciously, not quite sure whether to believe Jack or not.

"I know because I was a soldier on that ship," replied Jack.

The story frightened both Paul and Tommy, but intrigued them at the same time. Paul looked down at the murky water underneath his feet, then up to the black clouds that were strewn across the Linchester sky. "You said you thought there might be more bodies. What makes you so sure?" he asked.

"I believe that when Kilroy's skeleton was uncovered his evil spirit was unleashed. I think he is looking for revenge, and I think he is going after the families of the men who locked him in the hull," Jack replied.

Paul looked at Tommy and gulped, but as usual Tommy wasn't afraid. He was loving every second of the Kilroy story.

"By chance I was on holiday in Linchester and I read about the skeleton in the paper," continued Jack. "I went to the police and offered my help, but they said they didn't need it. I think they thought I was crazy."

"How do you know for sure that he wants revenge?" asked Tommy, trying hard to think of another reason.

"I know because I can sense it," said Jack. "I have psychic powers."

Paul giggled a little then quickly put his hand to his mouth to stop himself from laughing out loud.

Jack could tell that it wasn't only the police who thought he was crazy. "If you want, I can read your mind right now," he said to Tommy.

"Oh yeah," Tommy replied. "Go on then."

Jack looked straight into Tommy's eyes, not just looking but staring, without blinking or moving an inch. Slowly he started to turn his head from side to side, spooking Paul a little bit in the process.

"I know what you're thinking," Jack said. "You're wondering if I'm going to pay you for helping me."

"That's not true," replied Tommy.

"Yes it is," said Jack.

"Okay then, it is true. So how much are we getting?" retorted Tommy cheekily.

Jack smiled at Tommy's question. He liked it

when people were direct, just like he was.

Before Jack could answer, Paul stood up and started to walk away. Tommy quickly followed behind him.

"I don't care how much you're offering," shouted Paul over his shoulder to Jack. "I'm not chasing any ghosts for any amount of money."

"Are you sure?" Jack shouted back.

"Yes, I'm positive," replied Paul, very matter of fact.

"Ah well," said Jack, "that's a shame because I was going to give you both £500."

The words "£500" made Paul and Tommy stop dead in their tracks with their backs to Jack.

"Let's do it. Let's help him," Paul whispered to Tommy.

"I thought you were scared," replied Tommy.

"I am," said Paul. "Fear is fear, but business is business."

Both boys turned to face Jack. "We're in," they both shouted at the same time.

"Good," replied Jack. "We'll get to work straight away catching this ghost, then we can get rid of it."

"How will we get rid of it?" Paul asked.

"By using the one thing that Kilroy was scared of the most," answered Jack. "Believe it or not, although he was a ship inspector the guy couldn't swim. He was petrified of water."

"Well, how will we find him?" asked Tommy.

"It's not how are we going to find him," replied Jack. "It's where will his next victim show up."

Chapter 4

The Body in the River

The car horns blared angrily through the streets and across the rooftops of Linchester. Bumper to bumper the streets and motorways were jammed with cars. The traffic snaked back in all directions, from the massive imposing concrete shape of the Linn Bridge, through the city centre streets, between the tall office buildings and up the dark alleyways. Every street was filled with cars. Every car was filled with tired and frustrated men and women trying to get home from work. This was the worst traffic jam Linchester had ever seen.

This was the work of Kilroy.

Jack, Paul and Tommy had long since abandoned their car and set off on foot, making their way through the noise and smoke of the busy streets that had ground to a halt, struggling to be heard over the din of car horns. They knew that somewhere at the end of all this bedlam, they would find the next victim of Kilroy. They climbed over cars, pushed past people on the pavements and struggled through the crowds of angry people desperate to know what had stopped the busy traffic flow of cars across the bridge.

Eventually, Jack, Paul and Tommy made it to the foot of the Linn Bridge. The police had sealed off part of the road in the middle of the bridge with blue and white striped tape, creating an invisible wall to stop people from crossing into their crime scene.

"Look down there," shouted Tommy, struggling hard to be heard over the ear-aching noise of car horns.

In the middle of the River Linn, floating on the dense darkness of water and sludge, was a police boat.

Inside it, two divers sat on the edge, checking their oxygen tanks and preparing to go into the water. High above them two sections of the bridge that were normally closed tight together, holding the bridge in place like large razor-sharp metal teeth, had come apart.

The divers pulled their facemasks on, gave the driver of the boat a thumbs up and toppled backwards off the boat into the water. The water did not splash. Instead, the divers disappeared beneath the surface as if they'd just dropped into a pool of oil.

Dark clouds continued to hang over the whole of Linchester, watching and snarling at everyone and everything below.

Jack ushered Paul and Tommy to make their way up the bridge towards the section that had come apart. "I think we've found victim number two," shouted Jack.

Tommy and Paul did not disagree with him. In fact, both knew without saying anything that Jack was right.

They walked past the cars on the bridge that hadn't moved an inch for hours, since the sections had come apart, past red-faced drivers who looked as though their whole bodies were filled with rage, towards the police scene at the top. It was as if the evil that filled the air was bleeding into every man, woman and child, turning them angrier and more aggressive by the minute.

The Body in the River

As they reached the top of the bridge, the noise from the traffic seemed to die away, replaced by a cold wind that whipped around them, flapping the police tape and forcing them to pull their jackets closed to fight off the chill.

Paul looked over the side, down to the horrible murky depths below and the police boat beneath them. One of the divers appeared in the water at the side of the boat. Pulling off his facemask, he shouted to the driver: "It's no good. We can't see a thing under there. It's too dark."

The driver walked to the side of the boat and pulled the diver up out of the water and into the boat.

"Any sign of the car?" the driver asked him.

The diver slipped off his oxygen tank and placed it on the floor of the boat. "No," he sighed. "Whoever was in it ain't coming out of it. He had no chance."

Jack reached the police tape first. It was obvious from the tyre marks on the road that a car had skidded over the edge when the sections came apart and had plummeted into the icy water below.

"How exactly did those sections of bridge come apart?" Jack asked one of the policemen.

"Where did you lot come from?" replied the policeman, ignoring Jack's question because he was too concerned with how they had got up there in the first place. "This is a police matter," he continued.

Tommy slipped unnoticed under the tape and walked to the edge of the sections that had come apart. Upon closer inspection he noticed that the sections weren't worn and didn't show any signs that they had gradually come loose. It was as though someone had just pulled them apart suddenly.

Underneath the metal teeth on a section of concrete, the words "Kilroy was here" were scored.

"Excuse me, but you'll have to go back down the bridge. This is no place for a kid," said the policeman, placing a hand on Tommy's shoulder and guiding him back under the tape.

Tommy turned to face him. "Those sections aren't worn," he said, trying his best to sound every inch the detective. "Someone must have opened them on purpose."

The policeman looked down at Tommy, then suddenly burst out laughing. "Really!" he said through the laughter. "You're saying that someone just pulled those half-ton concrete blocks apart, eh? Who was it? Godzilla!"

Before Tommy could reply, Jack pulled him and Paul away and led them back down the bridge towards the traffic at the bottom.

"It was a freak accident," shouted the policemen after them, but neither Paul, Tommy nor Jack turned around. They knew it was no accident, because they knew it was Kilroy.

"They'll never believe the story of Kilroy," Paul said to Jack.

"I know," he replied. "If we're going to find Kilroy, we're going to have to do it without the police's help."

Although they tried hard not to show it, it was obvious that Paul and Tommy were a little bit shaken after what they had just seen.

"I think the poor guy who went over the edge in the car was Kilroy's second victim," continued Jack. "Probably a relative of one of the men who locked him into the hull."

Neither boy made any comment, but both

were beginning to think that the £500 they were being paid wasn't worth it.

"If this thing can pull apart the Linn Bridge," Paul thought to himself, "how are we going to be able to stop it."

"We will stop it because we have good on our side, and it only has evil," said Jack, obviously reading the doubt in Paul's mind, "and good always beats evil."

"I don't know," said Tommy, turning to look at the space in the bridge. "Evil is doing a pretty impressive job so far."

Jack stopped walking and looked up towards the clouds. His eyes narrowed as though he was trying to block out the light.

Paul noticed that Jack had started to breathe very heavily. "Are you all right?" Paul asked him.

"I can feel him," Jack replied. "Kilroy is about here somewhere."

Tommy looked at Jack, not quite knowing what to make of what he was saying. "Well where is he then?" he asked.

Before Jack could answer, a heavy rumbling, like thunder, blasted out from the clouds, and a voice said, "I am all around you, and I am watching you."

It was the voice of Kilroy.

"Show yourself," screamed Jack towards the clouds.

"All in good time," Kilroy replied. His voice echoed down from the sky and vibrated through the bodies of both Paul and Tommy.

Paul wanted to turn around and run, but somehow he could not move his legs. The voice of Kilroy had frozen him to the spot in fear.

Then suddenly, as quickly as it had appeared, the rumbling faded away, moving away from them across the dusky Linchester night sky.

Jack turned to Paul and Tommy who were still standing open-mouthed with shock. "Well," he said cheerily, "I think that went quite well. At least he knows we're on to him."

Paul and Tommy remained silent and open-mouthed. It wasn't until Jack turned and started walking back to the car that Tommy turned to Paul. "He's a fruitcake," Tommy said, nodding towards Jack.

"I know," replied Paul, "and we're working with him."

"And you're the best partners I've ever worked with," shouted Jack. Without turning around, he was reading their minds again.

"I hate it when he does that," Paul whispered to Tommy.

"Me too," Tommy replied.

"So do I," shouted Jack, giggling a little as he continued walking away.

Paul leant closer to Tommy so that he could whisper in his ear. "What have we got ourselves into?" he asked.

Chapter 5

Jack's Story

The flames from Jack's makeshift fire twirled in the wind. Crackling and dancing, they cast large black shadows of Paul and Tommy into the darkness of the shipyards and the derelict warehouses behind them. The day's events on the bridge were very much in the minds of both boys as they sat silently staring into the fire, pulling their jackets up around their faces to keep the cold night air from biting their ears.

Jack could sense that Paul and Tommy were not exactly as enthusiastic as they had previously been, certainly not Tommy.

His healthy appetite for adventure seemed to have left him after the voice of Kilroy had bellowed down at him from the clouds earlier that day.

Jack threw some more scrap wood on the fire

and sat down across the fire from Paul and Tommy. The flames lit Jack's face from the bottom, throwing the shadows from his cheekbones over his eyes, making him appear quite scary to the boys.

In the distance the *Kurdler* sat high out of the water. The moon behind it made it difficult to see anything other than the large black outline of the ship. For some reason the *Kurdler* appeared more quiet and still than usual, like a wild animal waiting to pounce on its unsuspecting prey.

Paul took one quick look at the ship and turned his head away swiftly.

"The ship can't hurt you, Paul," said Jack, trying to offer him some comfort and support.

"I know," replied Paul, trying his hardest to look tough and not frightened.

"Do you believe in ghosts, Jack?" asked Tommy.

Jack took a deep breath and stared long and hard into the middle of the fire, as though he was thinking of something in particular, something that had haunted him his whole life.

"I didn't," replied Jack.

"I don't either," Tommy added before Jack could finish what he was going to say.

Paul was glad that Tommy had cut in so quickly on Jack, because Paul could sense that a big "but" was just about to appear in Jack's words. And he was right.

"But," continued Jack, "my time on the *Kurdler* changed all that."

Jack looked at both Paul and Tommy and could see that another story of ghosts and awful goings-on on the *Kurdler* might not be such a great idea. Instead he decided to leave his particular stories and memories of the ship to another time when both boys weren't feeling quite so scared.

Paul pulled the collar of his jacket up to his face and moved closer to the warmth of the fire. He felt glad that Jack had stopped short of telling them why he now believed in ghosts, but at the same time he was curious to know what exactly Jack knew. It was like when something terrible happened in a scary film, and he would hide his face with his hands, then peek through his fingers because his curiosity had got the better of him and he had to see what was going on;

now Paul found himself scared to ask Jack to finish his story, but too curious just to sit there and wonder for himself.

"What happened on the ship?" Paul found himself asking before he'd even thought it through. It wasn't the first time that his mouth had started talking before his brain had time to think.

It was all the encouragement Jack needed to continue.

"Okay, you guys, listen up," he said in his hip American accent. "I'm going to tell you the story of the *Kurdler*."

Paul and Tommy could tell by the tone of Jack's voice that this story wasn't going to have a happy ending.

"During the Second World War, because of a shortage of ships, the *Kurdler* was used to transport American and British soldiers all over Europe to fight battles against the Germans," said Jack. "I've already said I was on the ship, but I haven't told you what I saw and heard while I was on it."

Suddenly Paul felt a cold sweat running down his forehead. He turned and looked around the shipyards behind him, at the vast unoccupied warehouses all around him, and into the dark petrifying outline of the *Kurdler*, sitting high up out of the water.

"Because there were so many of us in there," Jack continued, "a lot of the guys found themselves bunking down, right down in the bottom of the hull, in the part we called the dungeon."

"Did you sleep down there as well?" asked Paul, his voice quivering a little with the cold night air and fear.

"Yes I did," replied Jack, "a couple of times, but in the end I would rather stay awake at the top of the ship than sleep at the bottom."

"Surely it wasn't that bad?" Tommy asked him, not quite sure whether Jack was genuine or just exaggerating to try to spook him and Paul.

"Well, it depends on what you think is bad," Jack answered. "If bad means that at night you would be woken with the sounds of a man's agonising screams, with him weeping and wailing and scraping into the night, then yes, it was pretty bad."

Tommy looked at Paul, then turned back to

Jack. "Yeah, that's what I meant by bad," he replied rather sheepishly.

"It wasn't just the noises though," Jack went on. "It was the effect it had on the other soldiers."

Paul moved nearer to the fire. Jack's words had drawn him closer with curiosity and fear.

"What do you mean?" Paul asked him.

"Well," said Jack, "a lot of very normal, perfectly sane guys suddenly turned not so normal and sane after spending some time down in the hull. I believe Kilroy did it to them."

The light from the fire started to die away and fade, leaving only a warm red glow on the faces of Jack, Paul and Tommy, gathered around it.

Jack leaned closer to the boys, stopping just above the fire that separated them. "Did you know that the *Kurdler* has the worst safety and suicide record of any ship in the whole world?"

Without replying, Paul and Tommy simply slowly shook their heads.

"Every year," Jack continued, "for the past eighty years, four people have died as a result of suicide or by accident on that ship. As far as the story goes, it was four men who locked Kilroy in the hull, so every year Kilroy kills four people in return until he can get out and kill those responsible, or kill the next man in their families."

"That means there are still another two to go," said Paul anxiously.

"Yeah," replied Jack. "We've got to stop him."

"I've never heard so much guff in my life," shouted Tommy. Obviously, Jack's story had done little to change Tommy's view that ghosts and ghost stories simply didn't exist. "Come on, Paul, we'd better head home," he said.

Paul sighed and slowly got up from the fire.

"I'll see you two boys tomorrow," Jack said.

"Yeah, tomorrow," Paul replied, as he pushed his hands inside his pockets to keep them warm and ran to catch up with Tommy.

As he ran he could hear the sounds of his own footsteps echo through the dark empty warehouses and abandoned buildings. He stopped to turn and look at Jack, but when he turned around Jack had disappeared, and the fire that had burned so brightly and kept them warm from the cold had gone out, leaving only a small twirling line of smoke from the black charred wood in the centre.

"Hurry up, Paul," shouted Tommy. "We need to get home sharpish."

"I'm coming," Paul shouted back. Without turning around, his eyes were still scanning the waterfront looking for Jack.

"There's more to this whole story," he thought to himself, "and there's more to you, Jack. No doubt we'll find out in time."

Chapter 6

Victim Number Three

"A man was killed earlier this afternoon in Linchester's Botanic Gardens after a freak gust of wind shattered the glass ceiling of the indoor plant display."

The newsreader's words screamed in Paul's ears. He was on his way to the supermarket with his mother when the news came through on the radio. As horrific as the accident was, Paul didn't feel surprised, just a little scared and disappointed. He was scared because he knew that what had happened in the Botanic Gardens was not an accident – it was the work of Kilroy, and the man who lay dead on the floor was victim number three.

At the same time Paul felt disappointed. He had tried hard to help Jack to find Kilroy before he struck again, but he'd run out of time.

"What are you looking for?" asked Paul's

mother as he rummaged through the pockets of his jacket.

"My mobile phone," he replied. "I need to phone Tommy."

Paul's mobile tumbled from his inside pocket and landed on the floor of the car at his feet. As it landed it started to ring.

"I think Tommy's looking for you too," said his mother knowingly. His mother had a strange ability to tell who was calling before answering the phone.

Paul reached down and picked up his phone. A simple glance at the display confirmed that it was indeed Tommy.

"Hello," said Paul anxiously. The news of the latest victim had put him on edge a little.

"It's me," said Tommy at the other end. "Have you heard the news?"

"I'm in the car with my mum just now. We've just heard it on the radio," Paul replied, trying hard not to talk too loud and let his mother hear him.

"We need to get down to the Botanic Gardens," Tommy said forcefully, making sure Paul knew that whatever excuse he was thinking up for not going there was never going to be acceptable.

"I know," replied Paul, surprising Tommy a little. "What about our other friend?"

Tommy went a little bit quiet at the other end of the phone.

"What friend?" he eventually asked. Paul sighed with frustration. What Tommy had in terms of bravery was obviously making up for what he lacked in terms of brains.

"You know!" said Paul through gritted teeth. "Our other friend we met the other day, the one that's not from around here." Paul's mother turned to look at him, a little puzzled.

"Oh, that friend!" replied Tommy, finally realising that Paul was referring to Jack but couldn't say his name because his mother was sitting beside him in the car.

"I've got a funny feeling Jack will already be down there," said Tommy.

Paul smiled a little in agreement. He knew Tommy was right and that the chances were that Jack would already be down at the Botanic Gardens, sniffing around, seeing what clues he could find.

"I suppose you're not coming shopping with me," said Paul's mother. Paul turned to her with a sorry look on his face.

"Where do you want to go then?" she continued. "Tommy's house?"

"If you don't mind," replied Paul innocently and sweetly. His mother just laughed at his rubbish attempts to be cute.

"Fine by me," she retorted. "It just means you do all the dishes tonight on your own."

The image of cuteness that Paul had perfected gave way to misery at the thought of having to wash all the dirty pots and plates on his own.

"I hope you appreciate what I'm doing to help you, Jack Angel," he thought to himself.

Outside the car, the dark clouds continued to dangle in the sky, sagging in the middle as though full of rain and ready to burst, just waiting for the right moment to open up and soak everyone below.

The dismal light remained, gloomy and grey. It seemed that the whole of Linchester was lost in the dark and looking for someone to lead it to light once again.

It was almost an hour after they spoke on the

phone that Paul and Tommy eventually made it to the Botanic Gardens.

All the main entrances to the well-kept park had been closed by the police, leaving tourists to stand on the pavements outside, slightly confused and wondering what was going on.

Tommy pushed his way through them until he was standing directly in front of the gates at the mouth of the crowd. Two large police officers stepped forward to prevent him from getting any closer.

"Sorry, son," said one of them, "but the park is closed at the moment. There's been a bit of an accident."

Tommy turned and squeezed his way back through the crowd towards Paul who was standing waiting at the rear of them.

"Well?" Paul asked Tommy as he saw his head emerge from between two large tourists trying to see over the crowd into the park.

"No chance," Tommy replied. "The police have closed the whole of the park, and they're not letting anyone in or out."

"Is that so?" said Paul. A devious little grin crept across his face. "Well, I might just know another way in. Come on, follow me." Paul turned and ran down the pavement alongside the large metal black fence that surrounded the whole of the park with its trees, lawns and bushes. Tommy followed closely behind him.

Eventually Paul stopped at a section of the fence that had come loose, and, pushing the fence back slightly, he managed to squeeze through and hide in the bushes behind it.

"Aargh!" shouted Tommy, his voice attracting the attention of the policeman across the grass in another section of the park. Paul turned to see Tommy wedged between the two sections of fence. He hadn't pushed the loose section of the fence back far enough, and as he had tried to squeeze through it had swung back and squashed him between the two, like a mouse in a trap.

Paul jumped and pulled the fence back far enough for Tommy to slip through, holding his shoulder. "That was sore," he said loudly to Paul, not realising the volume of his voice.

"Ssshh," Paul replied, pointing to the legs of the policeman that were fast approaching the bushes they were hiding in. "Follow me."

Like a couple of undercover secret agents they made their way through the bushes and trees, away from the policeman to another area of the bushes where they could see the large glass indoor plant display. Slowly they lay down on their stomachs and crawled slowly to the edge of the bushes for a better look.

It was like a huge conservatory, with sweeping panes of glass for walls and a large jagged hole where the glass roof had been.

Outside, the police were coming and going. A photographer was taking photographs of the shattered ceiling from lots of different angles, and a large black van with the word "Coroner" sat parked near the entrance.

"Can you see Jack?" Tommy whispered.

"No I can't," Paul replied, "but I know he's here somewhere."

Paul looked back down the park towards the main entrance. He could see the tourists still standing outside, waiting for someone to tell them what was going on.

Then suddenly a twig snapped in the bushes behind them. Before they could both turn to see who it was, two large hands covered their mouths, muffling the faint screams of fear they were about to make.

"Hey, you guys," the voice said in a lazy American accent. "How did you get in here?"

Paul and Tommy turned around to see Jack kneeling behind them.

"You scared the wits out of me," said Tommy angrily.

"I thought you didn't get scared," Jack replied, teasing him.

"Have you managed to see inside the conservatory?" Paul asked him.

"I don't need to," replied Jack. "Kilroy has gone. He isn't here any more."

Tommy dusted some dirt from his jeans and got to his feet, still crouching so the police couldn't see him. "What makes you so sure?" he asked Jack.

"I can sense it," Jack replied. "Kilroy is somewhere in the city west of here. He'll try to hide somewhere he thinks people will be less likely to look for him."

"What, like a graveyard?" asked Tommy.

"Maybe a church?" said Paul.

"He would definitely want to be indoors, out

of the way," Jack replied, "so the most likely place would be a church."

Paul turned to Tommy and gave him a smug "I was right" smile. Tommy just ignored him.

"The visions that I'm getting are a bit clouded," continued Jack.

"I'm not surprised," said Tommy. "Everywhere is a bit clouded right now."

Jack looked down at Tommy with a frown. "I meant I can't see clearly where Kilroy is," he said. "I can see him somewhere old and cold, somewhere very big with an enormous steeple and a massive entrance hall."

All three sat thinking of where it could possibly be, before the answer finally jumped into Paul's head. "I know!" he whispered triumphantly, desperately trying to keep his voice down. "If it's west of here, old, cold, with a large steeple and entrance, it can only be one place."

"Where?" asked Tommy and Jack together.

"It has to be Linchester Cathedral," said Paul.

"You're right. It must be the Cathedral," Tommy added.

"Good," said Jack. "Now we must go there."

The joy at having worked out where Kilroy was hiding was short-lived for Paul. Suddenly realising that he would have to go with Jack to kill the evil spirit made him wish he'd kept his mouth shut.

"Time is running out," Jack said urgently. "We have to go now."

Jack got up and quickly and quietly made his way back through the bushes, followed closely by Tommy.

Paul slowly got up, dusted himself down and thought to himself "I think I should ask for a pay rise."

Suddenly Jack appeared back at his side and whispered in his ear, "I can hear what you're thinking, and the answer is no."

Paul looked at him for a few seconds without saying anything, then he replied, "Well, I'm glad we got the whole money thing sorted."

"So am I," retorted Jack. "Now let's move."

Chapter 7

Murder in the Cathedral

Large forks of lightning split the Linchester sky, cracking over Linchester Cathedral and down towards the large metal cross on the top of the steeple.

The clouds hung darker and blacker over the Cathedral, more than anywhere else in the city, constantly rumbling like a panther's growl as it works itself into a frenzy before attacking its next prey, but protecting whatever it was that lay inside the large wooden doors.

Darkness and night-time came a lot earlier in the evening. The wind whistled all around the Cathedral, whipping up leaves and dirt as if someone or something was using it as a protective shield, a warning not to come too close.

Sections and bricks from the roof lay in the courtyard around it. They had come loose as people had tried to get inside to pray, eventually forcing them back away from the Cathedral.

The rough edges of the large sandstone bricks threw shadows around the exterior walls like long black daggers, and all the while the lightning cracked, the clouds rumbled, the wind whistled and somewhere behind the doors, Kilroy waited.

Jack's long black car pulled up outside the Cathedral with Paul and Tommy inside. Their appearance only made the wind and the lightning worse, as if it was striking in anger at them.

Jack opened the door and stepped outside into the courtyard. His long black overcoat flapped furiously in the wind. The dust and the leaves that filled the air forced him to close his eyes to protect them.

Paul and Tommy appeared by his side. Paul looked up at the lightning that cracked across the sky in seemingly never-ending forks, threatening them, telling them to go back.

The clouds rumbled and rolled inwards, as though they were making a monstrous storm especially for the three of them.

By now the noise from the clouds and the wind had got so loud that Jack had to shout to be heard above it.

"Don't be scared," he yelled to Paul and Tommy. "This is just Kilroy trying to scare you."

Tommy looked up at the large steeple that towered above them. "Well it's working," he shouted back.

Paul looked at Tommy in disbelief. This was the first time he'd ever heard Tommy say he was scared of something.

Instantly Paul himself felt less afraid. He knew now it was his turn to be strong and brave, as Tommy had been for him so many times in the past.

Jack took Paul and Tommy by the hand, and slowly walked across the courtyard to the large wooden doors that led inside, fighting hard against the wind that tried to beat them back with every step.

As they drew closer to the door, the lightning struck the metal cross on top of the steeple, sending a shower of sparks down towards them. Jack pulled Paul and Tommy closer, shielding them from the hot sparks that were falling dangerously to the ground all around them.

The wind grew stronger. Its noise became deafening, hurting the ears of all three as they struggled on, fighting the wind, the lightning, the noise. Large chunks of the Cathedral's roof broke away and plummeted down to the court-yard below, crashing to the ground in front of Jack and the boys.

"Keep going," shouted Paul, "we're nearly there."

Jack threw out his hand and with all his strength pushed one of the large wooden doors open, then helped Paul and Tommy inside.

As Paul and Tommy turned to pull Jack in, the wind pushed him so hard that it lifted him off his feet, sending him crashing on to the cold concrete ground.

"Grab my hand," screamed Paul, leaning back out of the door with his arm outstretched.

Jack crawled towards Paul, the wind pushing his head down, the lightning striking in the skies above him, the clouds roaring at him in anger. He stretched out a hand and Paul grabbed it.

"Pull me back in," Paul shouted over his shoulder to Tommy.

Tommy grabbed Paul around the waist and, with all the strength he could find, yanked Paul and Jack through the door, sending all three of them falling to the ground.

With a heavy foot, Jack turned and kicked the large wooden door closed.

Then there was silence. Nothing. No noise. The wind had gone, the lightning stopped, the clouds were silenced.

"It's just us and Kilroy now, boys," Jack whispered to them, climbing to his feet.

Paul got to his feet and looked down the long entrance hall to the stairs that led into the church itself. The walls were light grey and dusty, and the entrance hall was empty.

"Look over there," said Tommy.

Paul and Jack turned to see the words "Kilroy was here" scratched on to one of the walls.

"He must be in the church," said Jack. "We'll have to go in and get him."

Paul took a deep breath. Slowly all three walked down the hall towards the door of the church. As they neared they could feel the air getting colder. The closer they got, the colder it became.

They reached the bottom of the stairs that led into the church, although there were only six large concrete steps, to all of them it seemed like a mountain to climb.

"Let's do it," said Paul to Jack and Tommy.

They didn't need to reply because they knew, like Paul, that now was the time they'd have to show more courage than ever before, confront their worst fears and walk into the church where the most evil ghost in the world would now be waiting for them.

Paul was the first to start climbing the stairs, followed by Jack and Tommy. As he reached the top Paul noticed a large marble fountain of holy water just inside the door.

As they walked through the door of the church the cold air hit them like a thousand needles in the chest. The temperature had dropped from cold to freezing.

"We know you're in here," shouted Jack, his deep American accent bellowing through the empty church, through the cold empty seats and down the long deserted aisles.

There was no reply.

"Maybe we got it wrong," said Paul.

"We got it right," replied Jack immediately. "I can sense him. He's in here somewhere."

The words had no sooner left Jack's mouth than a loud spine-chilling whisper filled the air around them. "Well done," it said. "You have found me, and because of this, you must not leave here alive."

Jack turned to Paul. "I think that was Kilroy," he said, trying hard to make light of the situation they were in.

Paul didn't reply to Jack. Instead he looked at Tommy. "The phrase 'stating the bloomin obvious' springs to mind."

Suddenly, high up in the corner of the ceiling at the far end of the church, Kilroy slowly moved out from where he had been resting.

His long thin pointy arms were wrapped around his body, his long narrow head was bowed beneath his shoulders. As he reached the centre of the church, slowly he lifted his head to show them his evil face. His eyes scanned Jack, then Tommy, but when his eyes locked on Paul, his face began to change. He rocked his head from side to side, a small evil smile creeping across his face as though he'd just been handed a gift. Then his expression turned to anger.

"You are the one," he screamed at Paul. His voice was so piercing and deafening that it shattered the glass in the large stained-glass windows in the walls.

Suddenly, his long arms shot out sideways, and in a flash he tilted his entire body towards Paul and swept down the church towards him.

"Get out of here, Paul," Jack screamed.

Paul turned and ran back down the church with Tommy.

"Take me," shouted Jack to Kilroy, but he swept past straight over his head towards Paul.

"Why does this always have to happen to me?" Paul asked himself as he ran, terrified, towards the door, with Tommy close beside him.

As he ran he could hear his heart beating fast in his ears. He got closer and closer to the door, then suddenly, he stopped.

Tommy ran another couple of yards before realising that Paul wasn't there, then skidded and turned.

"What are you doing Paul? Run!" he shouted.

Paul stood in the centre of the church. His breath could be seen in the freezing cold air as he gasped loudly. Then he turned to face Kilroy.

"If you want me, come and get me," he shouted. Kilroy stopped and hovered for a second in the air above him. Jack and Tommy looked on in disbelief as Paul just stood there, waiting for Kilroy's attack.

Then, from out of nowhere, Kilroy screamed a loud ear-piercing scream and flew towards Paul. Tommy closed his eyes, not wanting to look. Jack looked on in terror, and Paul just stood there, frozen to the spot.

Kilroy lifted his long thin arms above Paul, but before he could swing them, Paul suddenly jumped to the side towards the holy water fountain. He filled his hands with water, then turned and threw it straight into Kilroy's face.

Kilroy's agonising screams echoed around the church as he reeled back in agony. Then he shot up skywards and out of the door of the church. Down the long entrance hall he flew, his long thin body twisting and spinning in fear. The large brown doors flew open, whipping leaves and dirt inside, and quickly Kilroy disappeared outside, taking the leaves and the dirt with him like a vacuum.

The doors swung shut, and once again there was silence. No sound.

"That was a very brave thing you did," said Jack to Paul, who was still breathing heavily and in shock at what had just happened.

Tommy slowly walked towards Paul. "Are you okay ?" he asked him.

Paul didn't answer. Instead, he just nodded his head.

"Why was he after you?" Tommy now asked.

Paul looked at Jack, not sure what to say. He needed answers too, just like Tommy.

"The reason he came straight for you Paul," said Jack, "is because you're number four, the last victim he needs."

Paul closed his eyes. It was all too much for him to take in.

"Did your grandfather work in the ship-yards?" Jack asked him.

Paul nodded.

"Your grandfather didn't have any sons, only a daughter – your mother?"

Again Paul nodded.

"You don't have any brothers do you?"

Paul shook his head.

"You are the next man in your grandfather's family," Jack added. "That is why he came after you. Your grandfather must have been the fourth man who chased Kilroy all those years ago."

Paul slumped his tired dejected body to the floor and looked up at Tommy.

"Who would have believed it," Tommy said. "We were trying to find him before he found victim number four, and the whole time you were victim number four. There's only one thing to do now – we have to hide you."

"I'm not hiding from him," Paul replied. "If I run now, I'll spend the rest of my life running and hiding from Kilroy, and every time he will find me. I have to face him now."

Jack placed a reassuring hand on Paul's shoulder. "Don't worry Paul," he said, "We'll beat him."

"How will we find him?" asked Paul.

"We don't need to," Jack replied. "He'll come for you, remember. You're his next victim."

Chapter 8

Storm Over the Linn

"I don't know how I let you talk me into this," said Paul, staring down at the murky waters of the River Linn only inches away from him.

Paul and Tommy were sitting in the middle of the River Linn on a home-made raft they had built with Jack's help. It was small, it was unsafe, and it was the genius plan that all three had come up with to trap Kilroy.

Except now it didn't seem like such a genius plan to either of them. The wind had started to pick up, from a gentle breeze to a more blustery gust. The daylight had disappeared almost the instant that Paul and Tommy had placed their rickety little raft in the water. Now all that remained was darkness.

Tommy glanced over his shoulder towards the dark derelict warehouses at the side of the river. Everywhere was dark. Everything was somehow in a shadow.

The normal faint sounds of rats scurrying around looking for scraps had gone. Farther down the river the *Kurdler* remained, the place where it had all began so many years ago. The ship of horror where countless numbers of men had died in bizarre accidents or killed themselves after hearing Kilroy way down at the bottom.

The only man left to die now was floating in the middle of the river with his best friend, and at only ten years of age, Paul didn't feel like dying.

"Look what I've brought," said Tommy. "I've come prepared."

He reached inside his jacket and pulled out a large green and orange water pistol with the words "Master Blaster" written on the side.

Paul giggled a little before reaching into his own jacket and pulling out the exact same gun. "Great minds think alike," he said to Tommy before placing it back inside his jacket for safe-keeping.

"The only difference between our water pistols," continued Paul, "is that I've remembered to fill mine with water."

Even though he realised now he had forgotten to fill his up, Tommy still had a quick look at his gun in the hope that Paul might just be teasing him, so he wouldn't feel embarrassed. A quick glance told him his water level was empty.

"Oops," said Tommy, feeling a little silly as he leaned over the edge of the raft to fill his pistol up. The murky water lapped against the side of the raft, bobbing it and rocking it from side to side.

Tommy quickly filled his water pistol up and sat back beside Paul.

"Where do you think Jack is?" asked Paul.

Tommy shrugged his shoulders. "Why?" he replied. "You don't think he would just leave us here to confront Kilroy on our own do you?"

Paul looked at Tommy and sensed a little fear in his normally brave eyes. "No he wouldn't do that," he said. "Jack will show up, if he's not here already."

Although Paul wasn't sure himself, he didn't want to worry Tommy any more.

"Yeah you're right, he wouldn't do that," replied Tommy, looking around at the edge of the water. "How long have we been sitting here now?"

Paul looked at his watch. "It's just gone seven pm now," he said, "so we've been waiting for just over two hours."

The sudden realisation that both their mothers would be wondering where they were filled them with dread at the prospect of having to go home.

"Do you think Kilroy will come?" Tommy asked.

"I know he will come," Paul quickly replied. He knew himself that Kilroy would not stop hunting him unless they stopped him, permanently.

The wind had by now dropped in temperature, so Paul and Tommy huddled closer on the raft to try to shield themselves from the cold, biting night air.

"Listen, Tommy," Paul said. "Kilroy isn't after you. It's me he wants. If you want to get out of this now and just go home I would understand."

Tommy turned to look at Paul. "It doesn't matter which one of us he's after," he replied. "We're a team, so we stick together."

Tommy's words were exactly what Paul wanted to hear. Although Tommy was his friend and he didn't want anything to happen to him, he felt stronger with him by his side.

"You're the best friend I've ever had," Paul said quietly to Tommy, trying hard to sound macho and not soppy.

"I'm the only friend you've ever had," replied Tommy, poking fun at him.

"That's beside the point," said Paul.

Their laughter echoed out across the dark night sky as both of them fell backwards on the raft, giggling and laughing, forcing the unsteady raft to rock harder, threatening to tip them both into the freezing cold water of the River Linn beneath them.

Paul steadied the raft and pulled Tommy up so they were both sitting upright again. Tommy was still giggling as he got comfortable again, then, as quickly as he'd burst out laughing, his expression changed to fear.

"Look Paul," he said, gulping with fright, and

pointed across the water to the warehouses directly opposite them.

Paul slowly turned to look at them, and there in the middle of all the darkness, in the centre of all the abandoned and unoccupied warehouses, one warehouse was lit brightly from the inside, the light blinking through every window throwing shadows everywhere as an unearthly howl suddenly rose from inside it and filled the night air all around them.

Paul took a deep breath and turned to Tommy. "He's here," he said, his voice croaking with terror.

Suddenly the light vanished, as though someone had flicked the switch, and the warehouse was once again thrown into darkness.

The wind blew even more ferociously, rocking the raft as Paul and Tommy tried hard to steady it, then from inside the warehouse, the white, almost see-through, evil figure of Kilroy appeared.

Tommy quickly turned to Paul. "If Jack is here," he said, "now would be a good time for him to put in an appearance."

Kilroy loomed menacingly at the side of the

river, his long willowy white arms outstretched as they had been earlier that day in the church, just before he was about to attack.

His head rocked from side to side as he stared out at the boys in the middle of the water. "Paul," his evil voice shouted out towards them, "tonight is a good night to die."

Slowly and carefully, Kilroy moved across the top of the water, showing respect to the one thing below him that he knew could kill him.

As he moved the water blew into the air behind him, as though something was exploding underneath and forcing the water upwards. Kilroy opened his mouth wide, and an enormous gust of wind blew out from inside it, across the top of the water towards the boys, who sat petrified on the rickety raft. As it reached them it blew the raft high into the air, sending them headfirst into the icy water.

Paul was the first to resurface. Fighting hard to keep his head above the ferocious waves that Kilroy had created, he shouted for his best friend, "Tommy where are you?"

Tommy appeared behind him. Every time he tried to shout back, a wave would suddenly come over him, sending him spinning beneath the water once again.

"Where are you, Tommy?" Paul continued to scream, the sheer noise of the waves struggling hard to drown out his voice and him at the same time.

"Over here," shouted Tommy just as he took another hit from a wave and went under once again.

Paul spun around in the water just in time to see Tommy's hand disappear beneath the waves. Paul started swimming towards him, his hands and feet thrashing through the water as hard and fast as he could as he tried to reach him.

Above and just behind him, Kilroy hovered, his thin evil frame just inches from the enormous waves that he had created.

Paul reached the spot where Tommy had gone under and immediately dived beneath the waves to look for him, but the water was so murky that it was almost impossible to see. He swam deeper and deeper until, just beneath him, he saw Tommy's outstretched hand trying to grab him.

He reached down and grabbed Tommy's hand, then kicked with all his might, dragging Tommy back to the surface.

As they both broke the surface of the water, Tommy coughed and wheezed water from his mouth, gasping hard for a breath. Then suddenly the waves died away, the wind stopped blowing, the noise became silence.

"Jack!" screamed Paul. His voice echoed through the night air, through the darkness of the warehouses, and stopped at the *Kurdler*.

Kilroy spun his body forward so that his face was only inches from Paul and Tommy's. "No one is going to save you now," he whispered to them. "Now you are going to die."

"Oh yeah," shouted Tommy. "If it makes us as ugly as you, no thanks." At that Paul and Tommy pulled their water pistols from inside their jackets and fired two cannons of water directly into Kilroy's face, sending him spinning upwards as he reeled away from them screaming with anger.

Paul and Tommy continued to fire at him until eventually he climbed so high in the air that the water from their guns couldn't reach him, and he turned back towards them, his face filled with fury.

"Do you honestly expect to beat me with toys?" he bellowed at them both. "No one can stop me, I am Kilroy, and I must kill you."

He raised his long pointy arms to the sky, and brought with him two enormous waves that rose from the water at either side of him and just hung there. Every movement of his arms forced an immediate and exact movement from the waves, until Kilroy's arms could reach no higher.

Paul closed his eyes, took a deep breath and waited for the waves to drop and pull him and Tommy down below the water. Kilroy screamed, an evil, terrifying scream that shrieked through the cold night air, then he looked down at Paul and Tommy beneath him.

"Hold your breath," said Tommy, "and wait for the water to hit."

But before Kilroy could drop his arms, an enormous spray of water exploded from beside them, and Jack came rocketing from beneath the waves, up towards Kilroy, and grabbed him tightly, sending them both tumbling backwards towards the water. As they fell, the enormous waves that Kilroy had created came crashing down on top of Paul and Tommy, sending them plummeting beneath the water.

Kilroy's agonising screams filled the air as he and Jack hit the water and Jack dragged him beneath the waves. The water thrashed violently as Kilroy fought as hard as he could to get away from Jack's grasp, but Jack had him tight and continued to drag and pull him below the water.

Paul and Tommy were still holding each other tightly as the enormous waves that engulfed them continued to force them deeper and deeper. No matter how hard they kicked, they couldn't get themselves to the surface. Paul couldn't hold his breath any longer as he forced the last drops of air from his body, sending small bubbles from his mouth all the way to the top.

Tommy kicked harder and harder, and very slowly managed to force a path for both himself and Paul back to the top, but as they came crashing up through the water to the air, the waves that had been caused by Jack and Kilroy threatened to send them both to the bottom of the river again.

"There's the raft," Tommy shouted to Paul, who was gasping for air and couldn't answer him. "Swim for the raft."

Paul and Tommy heaved their tired bodies through the water towards the raft. Time after time, wave after wave forced them underneath, only for them to come back up again fighting for air. As they reached the raft, Paul grabbed hold of the side and pulled Tommy alongside him. Terrified, they clung on to the side, too tired to climb on top of the raft as they waves threatened to flip it and sink it.

As Paul tried to shield his head from the waves he felt a strong hand grab his shoulder and lift him out of the water and on to the raft. As he turned he could see Jack lifting Tommy the same way and pushing him on to the raft.

"Grab my hand," screamed Paul, but instead Jack just smiled softly at him and Tommy. "Kilroy is below us somewhere," he said. "I have to make sure he never comes back. You boys were very brave tonight. I'm very proud of you."

Paul and Tommy watched Jack disappear back below the waves. The water continued to toss and throw the raft for a few seconds, then it stopped. The enormous black clouds above them, which had filled the sky since Kilroy was unleashed, suddenly erupted with thunder and slowly rumbled back across the sky, down the river from where they had come. As they passed over Paul and Tommy clinging for their lives on the raft, small pockets of warm early evening sun spread across their faces, making them smile.

"Look, Paul," said Tommy, nodding towards the water below them.

The dark, dense murkiness had disappeared and now they could both see their reflections looking back up at them on the raft.

"Are you all right out there?" came a shout through a loud megaphone.

Paul and Tommy looked to the bank of the river, where a man in uniform was standing looking out at them.

"We're all right," Paul yelled back as loudly as he could.

"Good," the man replied. "This is the police.

Stay on the raft. We're sending a boat to come and get you."

"Oh no," Tommy groaned to Paul. "What will our mums say about all this?"

Chapter 9

The Truth About Jack

"You stupid, stupid boys! What on earth were you thinking of?"

It hadn't taken long to find out what their mothers were going to say. In fact, it took a little under an hour.

It was exactly what Paul had expected his mother's first words to be, as he sat resting on the bonnet of a police car at the riverside with Tommy. They had large grey police blankets wrapped around them to keep them warm. Their wet, sodden clothes lay in bundles on the ground beside them. In the middle of the river police divers were continually going under and coming back, and every time they surfaced they would give the same shake of their heads, indicating that they had found nothing, no one, no sign of Jack.

It was through the maze of policemen and

cars beside them at the riverside that they had spotted their mothers pushing their way through the crowd.

Paul and Tommy were both delighted and scared at seeing their mothers – delighted because they felt safe when they were around and scared because they knew somehow they would have to try to explain everything that had happened.

Paul's mother ran straight up to him and threw her arms around him, squeezing him so tight that he nearly stopped breathing.

Tommy's mother did the same to him.

"You stupid, stupid boys! What on earth were you thinking of?" Paul's mum asked them. Paul could only look at Tommy, not knowing what to say.

Both boys realised that unless Jack showed up to confirm their story, no one, not even their own mothers, was going to believe that they, with the help of a private detective from New York, had killed the evil spirit of a spiteful ship inspector called Kilroy, who was responsible for the strange accidents and deaths all around the city and whose last victim was going to be Paul.

"There's no sign of anyone down there," a voice said over Paul's mother's shoulder. Paul's mother turned around to see an elderly police sergeant with a very annoyed expression on his face.

Tommy looked at Paul. "He must still be alive then!" he said.

"Who must still be alive?" asked Tommy's mother, who by now was more than a little confused.

"According to your boys," the police sergeant continued, "they were in the water with an American private detective called Jack Angel, killing a ghost, except we can't find any bodies."

Even the tone of the sergeant's voice poked fun at Paul and Tommy's story.

"You won't find any bodies because Kilroy was a ghost and Jack must still be alive," said Tommy, trying desperately hard to convince every adult standing around him of the truth.

"Oh yeah," the sergeant replied. "I think I've found a man who might know your American friend."

At that he motioned an elderly shipyard security man to come over. The man was old and plump, and walked slowly towards the small circle of people gathered around Paul and Tommy at the side of the police car.

"This is Harry Watson," the sergeant said. "Harry has worked as a security guard at the shipyard for over fifty years."

Harry walked over to Paul and Tommy and stopped just in front of them.

"Actually, it's sixty years," Harry said, correcting the sergeant without looking at him. Instead his gaze was fixed on both the boys. "Are you the young fellas that know Jack Angel?" he asked them.

Paul and Tommy just nodded in reply.

"Was this guy kinda tall and thin?"

Again Paul and Tommy just nodded.

"Did he say he was a soldier on the *Kurdler*?"

Paul and Tommy had by now become a little excited, nodding their heads quickly, knowing Harry could confirm their story.

"Where did he say he was from?" he asked Paul.

"New York City," Paul replied.

"Yeah, I know that fella," Harry said.

"See, I told you so," said Paul, spinning around to his mother and the sergeant.

"Yeah, I know him all right," continued Harry. "He died almost sixty years ago."

Harry's words made both Paul and Tommy's hearts sink. Paul just looked at him, speechless, not knowing what to say and not wanting to hear anymore.

"He was killed as he walked off the *Kurdler* in 1944. A hammer just fell from the sky and caught him on the back of the head. If you ask me I'd say that ship was cursed."

Paul stumbled back against the car slightly. The idea that the whole time Jack Angel had been a ghost was just too much for him to take in.

"If you ask me," the sergeant said to both their mothers, "they built a raft, got into trouble on the water, and made up this whole story so they wouldn't get into bother."

Both Paul and Tommy looked at their mothers, staring deep into their eyes, looking for something that might just tell them that their mothers believed their story and knew that they were telling the truth.

"Well, their little story didn't work," Tommy's mother replied. "Just wait till we get them home."

Paul slid off the bonnet and slowly walked towards his mother's car. With his tired and weary legs, every step was a struggle to him. He had wanted to believe so much that Jack had survived the fight with Kilroy in the middle of the river, that he was still alive, but the whole time Jack was already dead.

Tommy quickly caught up with him and placed his arm around Paul's shoulder. "I guess this means we won't be getting our £500," he whispered.

Paul smiled a little, not really wanting to. "I guess not," he replied.

Chapter 10

The Boys' Reward

The trees that passed by Paul's window in the car seemed to go on forever. The sunshine glinted through them for the first time in days, for the first time since Kilroy had appeared.

The car journey home was not exactly a pleasant one. Both Paul and Tommy's mothers had made it quite clear they were absolutely furious with them both, and had told them to remain quiet for the entire road home.

Not that Paul and Tommy felt like a conversation. Both were finding it hard to choke back tears after learning that Jack had been a ghost all along, and the chances of meeting him again were pretty slim.

Instead, they just sat there, like two strangers on a bus journey, not quite knowing what to say to each other. It was Paul who finally plucked up the courage to try to whisper to Tommy.

Slowly he slid himself closer to Tommy on the seat.

"I think we were lucky, Tommy," he whispered, "that Jack asked us to help him. If we hadn't had his help Kilroy might have got me."

Tommy didn't answer Paul. Instead he just turned to him with a look of disappointment on his face.

"You don't get it do you?" Tommy asked.

Before Paul could reply, he continued: "Jack Angel didn't just ask us by chance. He knew all along that Kilroy would be coming after you, so he was trying to protect you, kinda like a guardian angel."

It was clear from the look on Paul's face that this was something he hadn't thought of, but he knew Tommy was right and that it made more sense.

"Do you really think so?" he asked Tommy.

"What are you asking me for – I don't believe in ghosts, remember?" replied Tommy with his usual cheeky little grin on his face.

"Oh yes," replied Paul, giggling slightly. "I forgot about that."

"I thought we told you two to be quiet," came

the stern-sounding voice from Paul's mother in the driving seat.

Paul had a quick glance up to see her watching him closely in the rear-view mirror, her eyes shifting around quickly to catch everything they might be doing or saying.

Paul slid back along the seat towards the window with his head bowed, not wanting to annoy his mother any more.

"I don't believe you, Tommy. What have I told you about scratch cards?" Tommy's mother shouted from the front passenger seat.

She had been going through his wet clothes and found two scratch cards in the back pocket of his jeans.

Tommy looked bewildered and totally unsure of what his mother was talking about. "What scratch cards?" he asked her. "I didn't buy any scratch cards."

"These scratch cards," she replied angrily, tossing them into the back seat beside him.

Tommy picked up the scratch cards and began to examine them just as his mother was warming up for a rant, just like mothers do.

"I've told you before," she said. "It's stupid,

it's illegal at your age, and it's a waste of money."

"It says here," Tommy interrupted her, "that we've won £500."

Suddenly the car fell silent.

"Both cards have won £500."

A large smile crept across the faces of both Paul and Tommy.

"It must have been Jack that did this," Paul whispered excitedly.

"Yeah," replied Tommy, "he did it!"

As the car sped through the streets carrying everyone home, Paul and Tommy were too busy arguing over what to do with the money for their mothers to notice the tall thin figure by the long black car at the side of the road smiling towards them.

It was Jack Angel. As he turned and walked towards his car, it slowly began to disappear. As he drew near it his tall frame turned around for one last look at the boys as they drove past. "No, boys," he said, smiling proudly. "You did it!"